W9-BUU-789

DATE DUE

NO 1 2 '08			
DE - 6 '08			
DE 3 0 '08			
JN 2 9 '09			
MR 3 0 '10			
MY 2 0 '10			
OC 2 0 '10			
MR 2 7 '11			
4/23/13			
OC 0 6			
12-08-13			
AP 2 2 '14			

WordBooks
Libros de Palabras

Animals
Los Animales

by Mary Berendes • illustrated by Kathleen Petelinsek

Published in the United States of America by The Child's World®
1980 Lookout Drive • Mankato, MN 56003-1705
800-599-READ • www.childsworld.com

Acknowledgments
The Child's World®: Mary Berendes, Publishing Director
The Design Lab: Kathleen Petelinsek, Design and Page Production

Language Adviser: Ariel Strichartz

Library of Congress Cataloging-in-Publication Data
Berendes, Mary.
  Animals = Los animales / by Mary Berendes; illustrated by Kathleen Petelinsek.
    p. cm. — (Wordbooks = Libros de palabras)
  ISBN-13: 978-1-59296-795-7 (library bound: alk. paper)
  ISBN-10: 1-59296-795-7 (library bound : alk. paper)
  1. Animals—Juvenile literature. I. Petelinsek, Kathleen. II. Title. III. Title: Los animales.
QL49.B5446 2007
590—dc22   2006103376

dog
el perro

fur
la piel

nose
la nariz

tail
la cola

tongue
la lengua

dog collar
el collar de perro

ball
la pelota

puppy
el perrito

bone
el hueso

food
la comida

3

cat
el gato

ears
las orejas

whiskers
los bigotes

kitten
el gatito

yarn
el hilo

4

fish
el pez

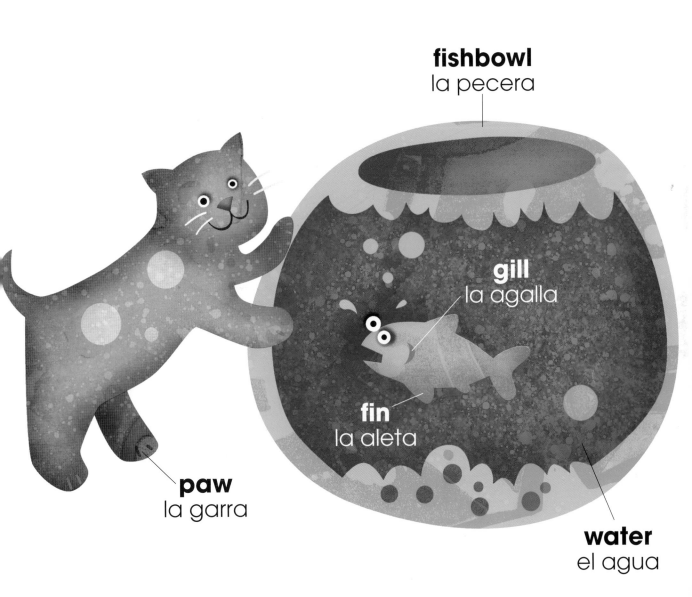

fishbowl
la pecera

gill
la agalla

fin
la aleta

paw
la garra

water
el agua

5

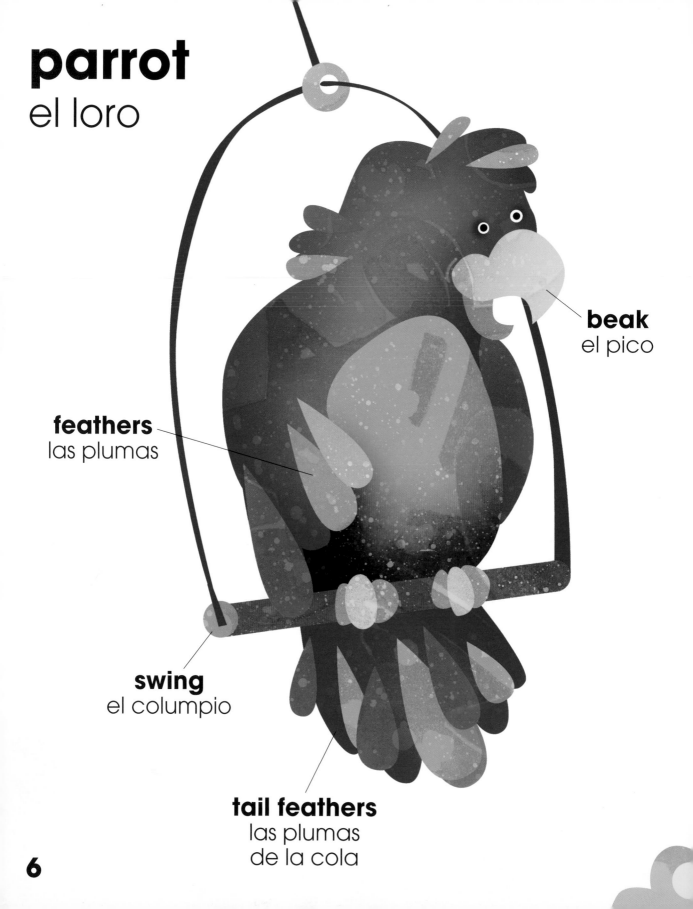

parrot
el loro

beak
el pico

feathers
las plumas

swing
el columpio

tail feathers
las plumas
de la cola

6

hamster
el hámster

hamster wheel
la rueda de ejercicio
para hámster

run
correr

foot
la pata

turtle
la tortuga

shell
el caparazón

log
el tronco

frog
la rana

fly
la mosca

lily pad
la hoja de
nenúfar

water lily
el nenúfar

pond
el estanque

crab
el cangrejo

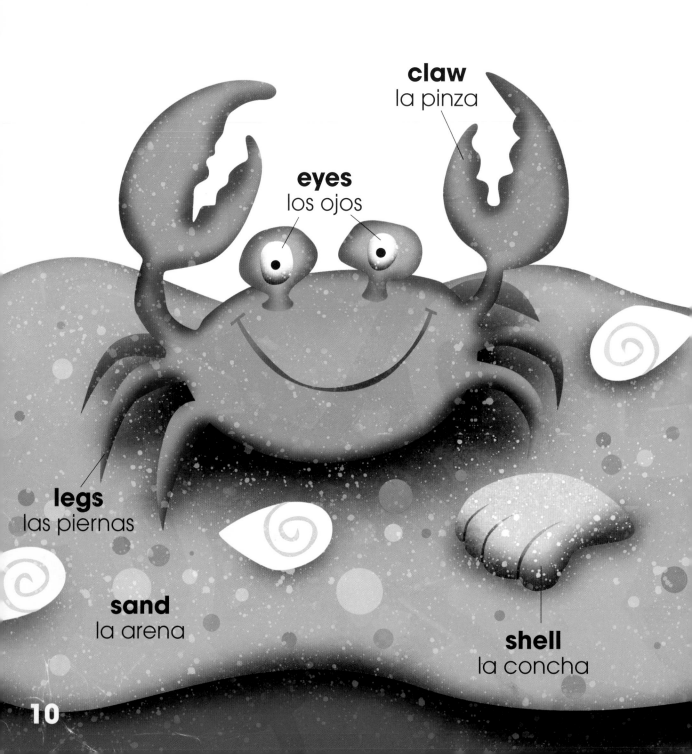

claw
la pinza

eyes
los ojos

legs
las piernas

sand
la arena

shell
la concha

duck
el pato

bill
el pico

ducklings
los patitos

webbed feet
los pies palmeados

swan
el cisne

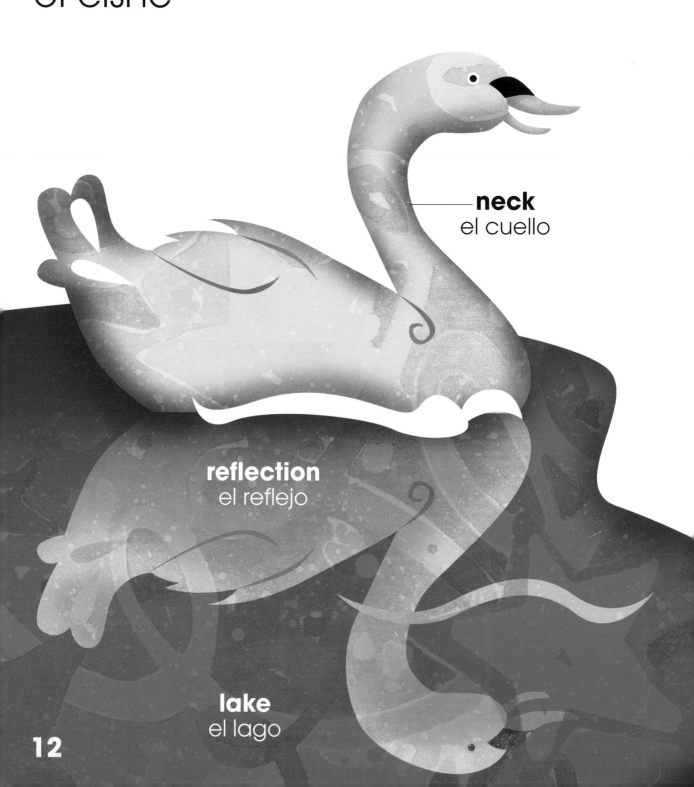

neck
el cuello

reflection
el reflejo

lake
el lago

sheep
la oveja

ears
las orejas

wool
la lana

lamb
el cordero

COW
la vaca

spots
las manchas

udder
la ubre

belly
la panza

nostrils
los agujeritos
de la nariz

horse
el caballo

mane
la crin

tail
la cola

hay
el heno

hooves
los cascos

15

rooster
el gallo

wing
el ala

chicks
los pollitos

feet
las patas

egg
el huevo

16

pig
el cerdo

snout
el hocico

tail
la cola

hooves
las pezuñas

17

bear
el oso

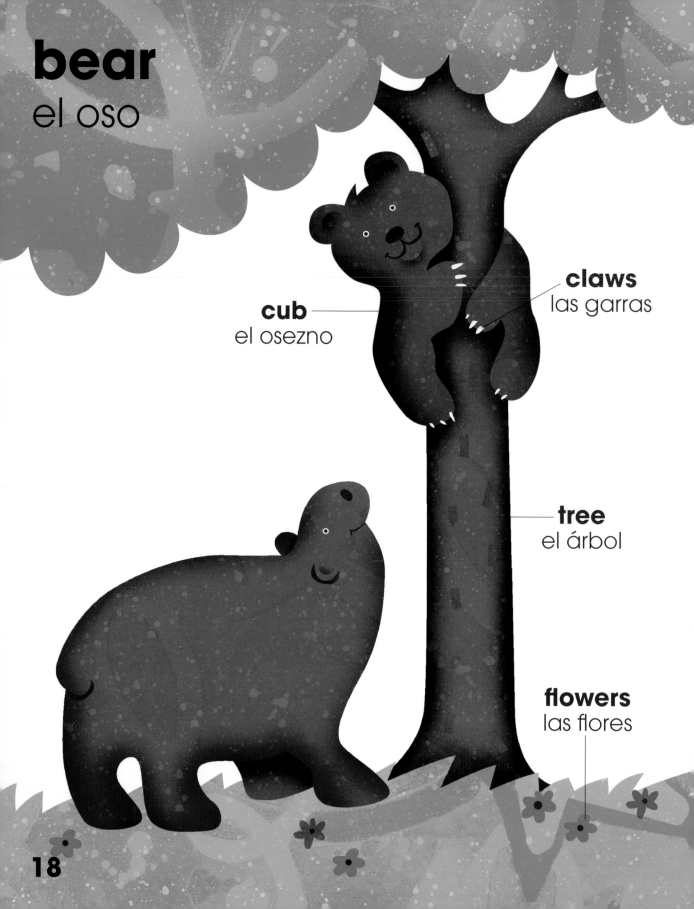

cub
el osezno

claws
las garras

tree
el árbol

flowers
las flores

18

deer
el ciervo

antlers
la cornamenta

bird
el pájaro

fawn
el cervatillo

grass
la hierba

19

raccoon
el mapache

mask
la máscara

branch
la rama

stripes
las rayas

20

rabbit
el conejo

ears
las orejas

cotton tail
el rabito
blanco

carrots
las zanahorias

21

fox
el zorro

kits
los cachorros
de zorro

sleep
dormir

den
la madriguera

owl
el búho

leaves
las hojas

stars
las estrellas

night
la noche

word list
lista de palabras

animals	los animales	**kits**	los cachorros de zorro
antlers	la cornamenta	**kitten**	el gatito
ball	la pelota	**lake**	el lago
beak	el pico	**lamb**	el cordero
bear	el oso	**leaves**	las hojas
belly	la panza	**legs**	las piernas
bill	el pico	**lily pad**	la hoja de nenúfar
bird	el pájaro	**log**	el tronco
bone	el hueso	**mane**	la crin
branch	la rama	**mask**	la máscara
carrots	las zanahorias	**neck**	el cuello
cat	el gato	**night**	la noche
chicks	los pollitos	**nose**	la nariz
claw (crab)	la pinza	**nostrils**	los agujeritos de la nariz
claws (animal)	las garras	**owl**	el búho
cotton tail	el rabito blanco	**parrot**	el loro
cow	la vaca	**paw**	la garra
crab	el cangrejo	**pig**	el cerdo
cub (bear)	el osezno	**pond**	el estanque
deer	el ciervo	**puppy**	el perrito
den	la madriguera	**rabbit**	el conejo
dog	el perro	**raccoon**	el mapache
dog collar	el collar de perro	**reflection**	el reflejo
duck	el pato	**rooster**	el gallo
ducklings	los patitos	**run**	correr
ears	las orejas	**sand**	la arena
egg	el huevo	**sheep**	la oveja
eyes	los ojos	**shell (conch)**	la concha
fawn	el cervatillo	**shell (turtle)**	el caparazón
feathers	las plumas	**sleep**	dormir
feet	las patas	**snout**	el hocico
fin	la aleta	**spots**	las manchas
fish	el pez	**stars**	las estrellas
fishbowl	la pecera	**stripes**	las rayas
flowers	las flores	**swan**	el cisne
fly	la mosca	**swing**	el columpio
food	la comida	**tail**	la cola
foot	la pata	**tail feathers**	las plumas de la cola
fox	el zorro	**tongue**	la lengua
frog	la rana	**tree**	el árbol
fur	la piel	**turtle**	la tortuga
gill	la agalla	**udder**	la ubre
grass	la hierba	**water**	el agua
hamster	el hámster	**water lily**	el nenúfar
hamster wheel	la rueda de ejercicio para hámster	**webbed feet**	los pies palmeados
		whiskers	los bigotes
hay	el heno	**wing**	el ala
hooves (farm animals)	las pezuñas	**wool**	la lana
hooves (horse)	los cascos	**yarn**	el hilo
horse	el caballo		